Lacey
the Little Mermaid
Fairy

A gift from the fairies to Lois Burrows

Special thanks to
Mandy Archer

ORCHARD BOOKS

First published in Great Britain in 2015 by Orchard Books
This edition published in 2016 by The Watts Publishing Group

3 5 7 9 10 8 6 4

© 2016 Rainbow Magic Limited.
© 2016 HIT Entertainment Limited.
Illustrations © Orchard Books 2015

HiT entertainment

A CIP catalogue record for this book is available from the British Library.

ISBN 978 1 40834 886 4

Printed in Great Britain

MIX
Paper from
responsible sources
FSC® C104740

The paper and board used in this book are made from wood from responsible sources

Orchard Books
An imprint of Hachette Children's Group
Part of The Watts Publishing Group Limited
Carmelite House, 50 Victoria Embankment, London EC4Y 0DZ

An Hachette UK Company
www.hachette.co.uk
www.hachettechildrens.co.uk

Lacey
the Little Mermaid
Fairy

by Daisy Meadows

Join the **Rainbow Magic Reading Challenge!**

Read the story and collect your fairy points to climb the Reading Rainbow online. Turn to the back of the book for details!

This book is worth 5 points.

Jack Frost's Spell

The Fairytale Fairies are in for a shock!
Cinderella won't run at the strike of the clock.
No one can stop me – I've plotted and planned,
And I'll be the fairest Ice Lord in the land.

It will take someone handsome and witty and clever
To stop storybook endings for ever and ever.
But to see fairies suffer great trouble and strife,
Will make me live happily all of my life!

Contents

Fairytale Castle

"I'm sure it's this way," said Rachel Walker, pointing to a twisty stone staircase. She lifted a rolled-up banner onto her shoulder and began to tiptoe down the steps.

Kirsty Tate followed behind her best friend. In her arms she was carrying a large cardboard box.

"This must be the east turret," she decided, stopping to peek out of an arched window. Rachel paused to look, too. From where they were standing the girls had a perfect view of the courtyard of Tiptop Castle. Kirsty beamed – it was like a scene from a fairy tale! A fountain carved in the shape of a shell bubbled merrily in the middle of the cobbles and

sweet-smelling pink roses curled up the columns around the sides. She wouldn't have been surprised to glimpse a royal princess wandering along the walkways or a knight ride in on a glossy white stallion.

"What a magical place," declared Rachel, "We're so lucky to be staying here!"

"I wouldn't have missed it for anything," agreed Kirsty, following her friend through an oak archway at the bottom of the stairs.

Rachel and Kirsty had been sharing an amazing spring holiday at Tiptop Castle. Being together was always a dream come true, but this week had been extra-special. The friends had taken part in the castle's annual Fairytale Festival. They'd spent their days dressing up in beautiful costumes, acting out stories and drawing pictures of all their favourite characters. Every night when the fun and games were over, the girls got to sleep in a real castle bedchamber! It was a world away from their homes in Tippington and Wetherbury – it was a place full of tapestries, glittering chandeliers and four-poster beds with velvet hangings.

The girls stepped out into the castle courtyard.

"The drawbridge is just over there," said Rachel.

Kirsty opened her cardboard box and lifted out the bunting inside. Every flag had been neatly stitched in rich crimsons and glittering golds.

"These would look really pretty pinned round the gatehouse," she suggested.

"Good idea," replied Rachel, unfurling her banner. She felt her heart skip when she read 'WELCOME TO THE FAIRYTALE BALL' twinkling in the afternoon light.

Kirsty and Rachel shared an excited smile. Tiptop Castle was celebrating the end of the Fairytale Festival with a wonderful party for all of the children who had taken part in the event. Their parents had even been invited to join in, too.

"All the grown-up guests will be here by six," said Rachel, tying the banner to the front gate so that everyone would see it.

Her eyes shone. There certainly was a tale to tell about this spring holiday! On their very first morning at Tiptop Castle, they had been visited by Hannah the Happy Ever After Fairy. The fairies were Kirsty and Rachel's very special secret. No one else knew about the magical adventures they had shared with Hannah and her friends.

Before they could say 'once upon a time…' Hannah had shrunk the girls to fairy size and whisked them back to Fairyland. They found themselves fluttering through the air to greet four beautiful fairies — Julia the Sleeping

Beauty Fairy, Eleanor the Snow White
Fairy, Faith the Cinderella Fairy and
Lacey the Little Mermaid Fairy. It had
been an honour to meet them, especially
when they'd presented Kirsty and
Rachel with a special book filled with
their favourite stories.

Rachel
shuddered
as she
remembered
what had
happened
next. When
she'd opened up

The Fairies' Book of Fairy Tales, all of
the pages had been blank! The Fairytale
Fairies had realised that their magical
objects were missing, plunging their

stories into terrible trouble. The magical objects were the invisible glue that kept the characters inside their tales. Without them, Cinderella and all the others would slip out and disappear.

It didn't take long to work out where the fairies' belongings had got to. With an icy blast Jack Frost had appeared, gloating with pleasure. He announced snootily that his goblins had swiped the Fairytale Fairies' objects so he could rewrite all of their stories in the way that *he* chose. Noble princes, fair princesses and kindly fairies were gone for good. Instead he cast himself and the goblins as the stars!

Before Kirsty and Rachel could do anything to stop him, Jack vanished to the human world. The Fairytale Fairies were dismayed. The Ice Lord had not only stolen their magical objects, he'd made off with all of their fairytale characters, too!

Ever since they'd got back to Tiptop Castle, Kirsty and Rachel had been trying hard to rescue the treasured possessions. They'd managed to return Julia's magical jewellery box, Eleanor's magic jewelled comb and Faith's magical shoe. They'd also helped the characters find their way back into the pages of *Sleeping Beauty*, *Snow White* and *Cinderella*.

"It really has been an adventure from start to finish," Rachel said.

"It's not over yet," Kirsty reminded her.

Rachel sighed. Poor Lacey the Little Mermaid Fairy was still searching for her magical object! If they didn't find it soon, the festival would be over and the story of *The Little Mermaid* would be spoiled forever.

"Come on," said Kirsty, slipping her arm through Rachel's and leading her back inside. "The decorating's done

now. Let's go and get ready for the ball."

The girls made their way across the courtyard, chatting about what to wear.

They skipped past the gurgling fountain, watching the sunbeams dance and glow in the water.

Rachel's heart began to flutter.

"Kirsty," she whispered. "Look!"

Kirsty had seen it, too. The sunbeams weren't sunbeams at all! Instead, a thousand tiny golden bubbles shimmered in the spray. The girls tiptoed up to the fountain, then sat on the stone ledge that

ran around the edge. There, in amongst the cascades, was a little fairy splashing about in the water! She looked up and smiled sweetly.

"Hello again!" she exclaimed. "Are you ready for an adventure?"

Mermaid in the Moat

Kirsty and Rachel recognised Lacey the
Little Mermaid Fairy straightaway – she
was just as pretty as they remembered!
Lacey's delicate wings glistened in the
sunshine and her mermaid tail shone
in sparkly lilacs and mauves. Her dark
hair was held in place with a fine golden

headband. Along the bottom of her crop top a row of tiny jewels glinted in the light.

"We're always ready to help a fairy," whispered Rachel, kneeling over the side of the fountain to make sure that no one else would see Lacey.

"Always," echoed Kirsty. "What can we do?"

Lacey's lovely smile faded. "It's my fairy tale," she sighed. "I can't go on for a minute longer without putting things right!"

"Is there still no sign of your magical object?" wondered Rachel.

Lacey shook her head sadly.

"What does it look like?" asked Kirsty.

"It's an oyster shell with a pearl inside," replied Lacey. "It's very precious.

The characters
from *The Little
Mermaid*
have been
gone for days
now. The
shell could
be anywhere!"

"We'll find it
somehow," promised Rachel.

"There must be somewhere new that
we can search," said Kirsty. "Let's
think…"

"Oi! Over here!"

Lacey and the girls looked up.
Someone was shouting from the other
side of the courtyard. Another voice
bellowed a reply:

"Well I never! Look at that!"

"It's splashing about all over the place!" yelled a third voice.

"Don't just gawp at it – let's get it!" boomed another.

Lacey flipped out of the water. "That noise," she cried breathlessly. "It's coming from the moat."

"We need to get there fast!" urged Rachel.

Kirsty began to run, but Lacey shook her head.

"You'll be faster as fairies," she said, pointing her wand into the fountain. As soon as the wand touched the water, a wave of miniature golden shells showered in all directions. Lacey beckoned for the girls to put their hands underneath it. Kirsty and Rachel gazed in wonder as the shells tickled and popped on their fingers before disappearing into the spray. Soon the girls were covered in a sparkling mist of gold.

"We're getting smaller!" exclaimed Kirsty.

When the mist cleared, Rachel reached up to touch her shoulders. A gauzy pair of fairy wings had appeared. The friends joined hands, then fluttered into the air.

"Oi, you!" shouted the voices again. "Come 'ere!"

Kirsty, Rachel and Lacey flitted across the courtyard, following the noisy shouts. They flew out past the gatehouse, across the drawbridge and over the moat.

"Oh my!" gasped Lacey, nearly tumbling out of the sky. "Goblins!"

Kirsty and Rachel looked down. Floating on the moat, in amongst the lily pads, was an inflatable lilo. Four green goblins were scrabbling around on it, fighting over a giant fishing net.

"She's too heavy!" moaned one goblin, tugging the net with all his might.

"Let me have a go," barked another, shoving his friend out of the way. The goblin heaved and hauled the net until – *plop!* – it landed on the lilo. The rest of the gang hooted in delight. A mermaid suddenly popped her head out of the net, then sat up in the middle of the lilo.

Lacey gasped. "It's the Little Mermaid from my fairy tale!"

"Trust the goblins to be up to mischief," frowned Rachel.

"Why did you do that?" asked the Little Mermaid, pointing at the biggest goblin. "It's not very nice – I don't like being fished out of the water."

The rude creature stuck his tongue out at her. "We don't care what *you* like," he announced. "We only care about what Jack Frost likes. And he's got a job for you."

The Little Mermaid looked puzzled.

"If he's going to be the star of your fairy tale, he'll need some mermaid lessons," added another goblin, "and who better to teach Jack Frost than the Little Mermaid herself?"

With that, the goblins erupted into whoops of laughter.

They sat clutching their sides, guffawing at their own cleverness. The Little Mermaid tried to talk to them, but no one would listen to a word she said.

Kirsty flew ahead of Rachel and Lacey.

"We must get down to the lilo," she urged, leading the way down to the water's edge.

"We'll have to be careful," warned Lacey.

The brave fairies made their way across the moat, fluttering from lily pad to lily pad. When they got close, they flew up beside the Little Mermaid.

"Shh," whispered Rachel, waving hello. "We're here to set you free."

The Little Mermaid looked at them with relief. "Thank you," she smiled.

"Now, if I can just wriggle out of this net…"

Kirsty tugged at the cords, but they wouldn't budge. They were wound tight around the mermaid's tail.

"It won't come off," sighed Lacey, pulling from her end.

Rachel frowned. The Little Mermaid was well and truly caught.

Just then, a huge paddle plunged into the water. Another one dropped down on the other side. The Little Mermaid leant over the side of the lilo, her eyes filled with worry.

"The goblins are rowing away," she whispered urgently. "What am I going to do?"

Lacey watched nervously as the lilo lurched downstream.

"We'll find a way to save you somehow," she called helplessly. "Oh, I do hope that we will!"

Search and Rescue

Kirsty, Rachel and Lacey flew after the Little Mermaid. The silly goblins were so busy paddling, they didn't notice a thing.

"Hurry up!" bellowed the biggest one, nudging his mate in the tummy. "We can't keep Jack Frost waiting!"

"He's going to have to," grumbled the other one. "How am I supposed to row any faster with a great lump like you weighing us down?"

While the goblins squabbled, the Little Mermaid wriggled about inside the fishing net. Her face fell when the lilo veered out of the moat and into a narrow sidestream.

"They're heading for Tiptop Pond," murmured Rachel, pointing to a pool of water hidden amongst the trees.

As the Little Mermaid and the goblins rounded the final bend, an old wooden boathouse loomed into view. Kirsty and her friends fluttered into the branches of a willow tree to see what would happen next.

Bang! Clatter!

The boathouse doors were suddenly flung open. The fairies watched in amazement as Jack Frost strutted into view. The Ice Lord was decked out

in a mermaid outfit and
swimming hat! He had
water wings on his
arms and a rubber ring
around his middle that
kept slipping down.
Big green toes poked
out of the bottom of
the costume where
the mermaid's
tail should have

been. He clutched a trident in one hand,
dripping with gemstones and gold chains.
Before Jack spoke to the goblins, he
couldn't resist peeking into the water to
look at his reflection one more time.

"Splendid," he preened, turning round
to admire the sequins that glittered all
over the outfit in icy shades of blue. He

swaggered up and down the bank of the pond, waiting for the goblins to notice him. When they didn't, Jack's face broke into an angry scowl. "Get over here now!" he bellowed.

The goblins paddled so hard, the lilo nearly tipped over.

"We got her, Your Majesty," squawked the biggest one. "The Little Mermaid."

Jack Frost banged his trident on the ground. The net instantly fell away from the Little Mermaid's tail. She flipped herself into the water, but there was no escape. The goblins made sure that they were blocking the stream that led back to the moat.

"You can leave when you've taught me what I need to know," declared Jack

Frost. "I want to act like a mermaid!"

The Little Mermaid glanced up at Lacey, Kirsty and Rachel. She had no choice. With a big sigh, she began the first lesson.

"We'll start with swimming and tail swishing," she decided. "You do know how to swim, don't you?"

"Humph!" muttered Jack Frost. He made a cross face, then gingerly stepped into the water, still clutching the trident in his fist.

Kirsty waited until the Ice Lord was in up to his waist. He tried to do swimming strokes with his arms, but his feet stayed rooted to the ground.

"Let's look inside the boathouse," she suggested. "Jack Frost could be here for hours!"

One by one, the fairies silently glided towards the shallow edge of the pond. Only the Little Mermaid noticed them go by, doing her best to make sure that Jack Frost faced the other way.

It didn't take long to search the boathouse. The magical oyster shell was nowhere to be seen. The fairies flew back outside, landing gently in a patch of reeds.

"What do we do now?" wondered Rachel, peeping across the pond. All the friends could see from their hiding place was the tip of Jack Frost's trident wobbling as he moved.

"He'd swim much better if he put it down," said Kirsty, absent-mindedly.

Lacey suddenly gasped in surprise. "Look!" she cried, pushing the reeds to one side. There, in amongst the priceless gems hanging from the trident, was her magical oyster shell with the pearl inside!

"No wonder he wants to keep the trident close," marvelled Rachel.

The Little Mermaid nodded happily, then whispered a fairy spell:

41

An oyster shell, a creamy pearl,
Bubbles gather, bubbles swirl!

Three foamy gold bubbles suddenly
rose out of the pond and floated
dreamily through the air. Kirsty and
Rachel beamed with delight
as the bubbles got closer
and closer to their heads.

"When they touch
you," said
Lacey, "dive
into the
pond.
The
bubbles
will help
you."

Kirsty and
Rachel did as

they were told. Suddenly they felt the bubbles settle on their heads. Instead of popping, they sat on their shoulders like pearly diving helmets.

"We can breathe underwater!" gasped Rachel, diving after Lacey. She looked back through the emerald green pond, but Kirsty was nowhere to be seen.

Suddenly a voice rang out in the shallows.

"Help me, someone!" cried her best friend. "I'm stuck!"

Tickle Time

Rachel and Lacey swam back as fast as they could, a little trail of golden bubbles streaming behind them.

"Over here!" cried Kirsty.

Rachel peered through the dappled water. There was nothing to be seen to the left or right, and only a thick clump of pondweed below. She looked again.

There was poor Kirsty, stuck right in the middle of it! Somehow the fronds had got wrapped around her arms and legs, holding her fast. Lacey reached into the weeds to grab her hand, but they began to tangle up around her, too.

"Don't come any closer," urged Kirsty. "You must get to the trident."

"We're not leaving you," declared Lacey, looking around for help.

"Let's ask those fish!" suggested Rachel.

A shoal of silvery fish with see-through tails glided in and out of the pondweed, nibbling at the stems. As soon as Rachel got close, they darted off in a hundred different directions.

"Please don't be scared," said Lacey. "We won't hurt you – we're fairies."

Slowly and nervously, the fish nudged their way back into the light. The moment they saw Lacey's friendly face and fairy wings they surged forward, swishing their tails excitedly.

Lacey said hello and pointed down to Kirsty. "This pondweed is so sticky," she explained. "She's tied up in knots."

"We can help," grinned a tiny fish with glimmering scales. "We're small, but we're very good at nibbling!"

With that, he darted down into the shadows and started munching on a pondweed branch. The others all joined in, too.

"That's better!" exclaimed Kirsty, as the stem around her arm broke free. She smiled happily as the fish nibbled the weeds on the other side, too.

"I'll dive down to the lower stems," cried another fish.

"I hope you're not ticklish," piped up a fish with bright eyes.

Kirsty started to giggle. The fish were nibbling the clump of pondweed wrapped around her feet.

"Oh my!" she chuckled. "I think I am!"

Working together, the shoal of fish nibbled Kirsty free in no time.

"Good work!" laughed Lacey.

Rachel's eyes began to twinkle. The fishes' speedy rescue plan had just given her a magical idea…

A few moments later, the fairies and their new friends were swimming through Tiptop Pond.

"This way!" called Rachel, pointing to a sandy spot not far from the middle.

The fish darted through the water. The silvery shoal seemed to move as one big fish instead of lots of tiny ones. They gathered in clusters around a twinkly blue column – Jack Frost's legs!

Lacey gave the signal with her wand. "One, two, three... nibble!"

The shoal flitted down to the pond floor, then started tickling and nudging at Jack Frost's pointy toes.

"Aarggh!"
There was
a dreadful
commotion
above the
surface.
Jack leapt
from foot to
foot, walloping the
water with his fists. The goblins watched aghast as their master erupted into shrieks of laughter.

Underneath the water Kirsty, Rachel and Lacey held hands, desperately hoping that Jack's attack of the tickles might cause him to drop his precious trident.

"It's no good," frowned Rachel. "He's not letting go!"

"We can't give up!" called Kirsty, swimming down to add some extra tickles of her own. Lacey joined in, but the Ice Lord still clung to the trident.

Rachel was just about to dive in, too, when Jack Frost glanced down. He spotted the fairies and his face filled with rage.

"What are you doing here?" he thundered. "I'm trying to have a mermaid lesson!"

Lacey summoned up all her courage and popped her head out of the water.

"I'm here for my magical oyster shell," she retorted. "Please give it to me!"

Jack Frost threw his head back and howled with glee.

"This little thing?" he smirked, lifting the trident out of the pond so no one else could reach it. "Well, I want it, so bad luck! You'll never get it back, not now and not ever!"

Fairytale Emergency

Lacey's wings drooped and her cheeks turned pale.

"What shall I do?" she sobbed forlornly. "My fairy tale will never be the same again!"

The warm golden glow that usually shone around the Little Mermaid Fairy had seeped away to almost nothing.

Kirsty and Rachel paddled through the gloom to get to her and gave her a big hug.

"Don't be sad. We never give up on a friend," promised Rachel.

"That's right," agreed Kirsty. She called out in a cheerful voice, "Keep tickling, fish!"

Jack Frost held the trident up as high as he could, but it was getting hard to keep his balance. Splashes rippled through the pond as he wobbled backwards and forwards. He hooted with giggles, slapping his spare hand through the water to shoo away the fish.

Rachel spotted a broken-off piece of reed floating down to the pond bed. She reached out and grabbed it.

"We've tried the feet," she decided, "so

let's move on to the knees!"

Rachel swam up behind Jack Frost, then gently touched the back of one knee with the reed. The Ice Lord's legs buckled and kicked – she'd found his ticklish spot!

"Get off!" roared Jack, flailing about like a jumping bean.

Splash!

The trident fell out of his hands, plunging the gems, chains and magical oyster shell into the water.

"Goblins!" screeched Jack, turning to
the lilo. "Get over here now!"

"We're coming, boss!" yelled the
biggest one. "Get a move on, crew – row
in a starboard direction!"

The goblin sitting beside him in the
lilo scratched his head. "That's forwards,
right?" he wondered gormlessly, turning
to his mate behind.

His mate nodded, then changed his
mind. The goblins began to paddle
furiously – in different directions! The

lilo moved nowhere at all. While Jack
Frost's servants flapped and splashed in
the water, someone else swooped in and
plucked the trident off the pond bed.

"I think this belongs to you," beamed
the Little Mermaid, offering it to Lacey.

Lacey's face burst into a dazzling,
delighted smile. Quick as a flash she
swam up and lifted the special shell
off the trident's fork. The instant the
fairy touched it,
the magical
object shrank
back down
to miniature
proportions.
Lacey prised open
the shell and peeped
inside – the oyster was still there!

"Well done," she gushed, reaching out to her friends. "We did it after all!"

"Thank you, Kirsty and Rachel," piped up the Little Mermaid. With a farewell wave she was gone, shimmering back into the pages of her story.

Now that her fairytale characters were back where they belonged, Lacey could sparkle again! She flipped and danced in the water, golden fairy dust fizzing all around her.

"I'm so pleased that you were here to save the day," she cooed gratefully, taking Kirsty and Rachel's hands.

"We are, too!" agreed the best friends.

Just then, a booming voice thundered across the pond. Jack Frost! He pinched his nose with a bony finger and plunged his face into the water.

"I am definitely *not* pleased!" he snapped. "You ruin everything!"

The smallest fish from the shoal nudged Rachel with his fin.

"I think Jack Frost needs more knee tickles," he suggested. "Don't you?"

Jack Frost spluttered with rage, then tried to stomp back to the boathouse.

61

Dozens of silvery fish followed behind him, nibbling at his knees.

"Don't go that way…" called Kirsty, her eyes twinkling cheekily.

"…it's full of pondweed!" finished Rachel.

Jack was in no mood to listen to anyone. The tickly fish were driving him potty and his mermaid outfit was getting harder and harder to walk in. He took another step forward, straight into the clump of slimy pondweed. Jack Frost fell backwards into the water, landing with a mighty splash.

Kirsty, Rachel and Lacey dissolved into giggles.

"Now," decided Kirsty, "it's nearly time for us to get ready for the ball."

Lacey nodded enthusiastically and opened her eyes wide. "May I ask you one last thing?"

Kirsty and Rachel both nodded.

"Will you come with me to Fairyland first?" asked Lacey. "There's a surprise waiting for you!"

A Fairytale Ending

Kirsty and Rachel's journey to Fairyland took place in the blink of an eye. The very second they left, time stopped in the human world. In that magical moment Lacey whisked the girls back to Fairytale Lane, the little winding street where she and the rest of the Fairytale Fairies lived. Julia, Eleanor and Faith were all waiting to greet them, plus two very important

royal guests. Kirsty and Rachel flushed
with pride – King Oberon and Queen
Titania were standing on the cobbles,
flanked by a smart row of frog footmen!

"Good afternoon, Your Majesties," the
girls said politely, bobbing down into
curtseys.

The queen smiled at them. "Our
heartfelt thanks is due yet again," she

said warmly. "You've put the magic back into our fairy tales. Now children everywhere can enjoy these wonderful stories once more."

King Oberon nodded regally, then beckoned for Kirsty and Rachel to walk with him. "We'd like to repay your kindness," he continued, "with a small kindness of our own."

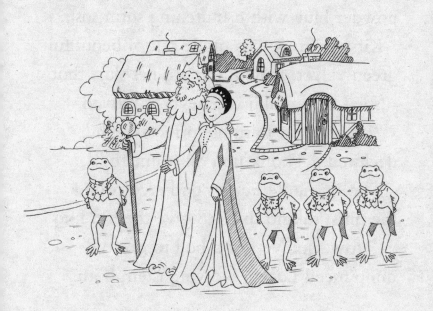

The king came to a stop outside Faith the Cinderella Fairy's house. Her Fairy Godmother opened the front door.

"These are for you," she announced, holding out two beautiful ballgowns. "I know you'll look spellbinding in them!"

"They're exquisite," gushed Rachel, holding her dress up for size. It was a chiffon gown stitched in the softest powder blue with a matching satin sash.

Kirsty's frock was made out of beautiful green velvet. It had a floaty net skirt that rustled beautifully whenever it moved.

"I feel like a fairytale princess!" she declared. "Thank you all so much."

The Fairytale Fairies gathered round the girls, taking turns to give them a hug.

"Now, you've got a ball to go to," announced Lacey, blowing them both a fairy kiss. "Have a magical evening. Goodbye, Kirsty. Goodbye, Rachel!"

With a flurry of sparkles and fairy dust, the visit was over. A little while later, the girls stepped into the Tiptop Castle ballroom. The Fairytale Ball was about to begin!

Kirsty looked down. She was already wearing the new ballgown from Cinderella's Fairy Godmother! Her hair was curled into ringlets and it glittered with diamantés.

Rachel looked lovely too, the blue gems on her dress matching her eyes perfectly.

"Are you ready?" she giggled. "Let's dance!"

The girls made their way over to the dance floor, holding their skirts up with their hands. Over at the banqueting table, Mr and Mrs Walker and Mr and Mrs Tate were chatting and nibbling party food. As soon as they spotted the girls, they gave them a big wave.

The music began to play, and Kirsty and Rachel felt like princesses again. They whirled and twirled round and round on the dance floor all night long.

"I don't want the week to end," sighed Kirsty.

Rachel nodded. "It really has been an enchanting holiday, hasn't it?"

Rosie, one of the festival organisers, thanked everyone for coming and pointed up to the ceiling. Suddenly, hundreds of golden balloons floated onto the dance floor! The guests whooped and cheered, batting balloons into the air around them.

"It's been a magical party," said Rosie, "and I can only think of one way to round it off…with a bedtime story!"

"We've got the perfect book," said Kirsty, putting up her hand.

"Oh yes," added Rachel. "May we go and get it?"

Rosie thought it was a wonderful idea. She spread out blankets on the ballroom floor and helped the children to snuggle up together. Kirsty and Rachel dashed up to their tower bedroom to fetch *The Fairies' Book of Fairy Tales*.

"Here it is," said Kirsty, lifting the sparkly book off the shelf.

"We've got a minute or two," whispered Rachel. "Let's take a look inside."

Kirsty opened the front cover and then flicked through the pages. All their favourite fairy tales were there, told in magical words and pictures. Near the end of the book, the friends came across a wonderful ocean scene. It showed a fine galleon sailing on a moonlit night.

"There's the Little Mermaid!" beamed Rachel, pointing to the water.

Kirsty was thrilled to see her back where she belonged.

"What a wonderful week with the fairies," she gasped. "It's been an adventure from start to finish!"

"Yes," agreed Rachel, "an adventure with a fabulous, fairytale ending!"

Meet the
Fairytale Fairies

Julia
the Sleeping Beauty
Fairy

Eleanor
the Snow White
Fairy

Faith
the Cinderella
Fairy

Lacey
the Little Mermaid
Fairy

Kirsty and Rachel are going to a Fairytale Festival!
Can they help get the Fairytale Fairies' magical objects
back from Jack Frost, before he ruins all the stories?

www.rainbowmagicbooks.co.uk

Now it's time for Kirsty and
Rachel to help...

Frances the Royal Family Fairy

Read on for a sneak peek...

Two magical invitations from Fairyland
were lying on Kirsty Tate's bed. As she
and her best friend Rachel Walker got
dressed, they both kept glancing at the
invitations. The delicate green leaves
glimmered with swirly golden writing:

*Princess Grace and Prince Arthur are
delighted to announce the birth of their
second child. A beautiful sibling for
Prince George!*

*You are invited to celebrate the new
arrival and attend a welcoming ceremony
at the Royal Fairyland Palace.*

Someone special will collect you both
at midday on Saturday!

"We are so lucky," said Rachel, pinning a sparkling flower clip into her hair. "This will be the second royal baby ceremony we've attended."

"I wonder if it will be like Prince George's ceremony," said Kirsty, remembering that special day. "Hopefully Jack Frost has behaved himself this time!"

Before Prince George's naming ceremony, naughty Jack Frost and his mischievous goblins had stolen Georgie the Royal Prince Fairy's royal seal. The girls smoothed down their frilly skirts and smiled at each other. They had been so excited when the invitations wafted through their bedroom windows three days ago. It was always exciting to get a message from their fairy friends, but a royal ceremony was very special indeed.

Kirsty brushed her glossy hair and then laid her hairbrush down on the dressing table.

"Well, we're ready," said Rachel, looking at her watch. "It's almost midday. Who do you think is coming to collect us? Will it be Georgie?"

Read Frances the Royal Family Fairy to find out what adventures are in store for Kirsty and Rachel!

Calling all parents, carers and teachers!
The Rainbow Magic fairies are here to help
your child enter the magical world of reading.
Whatever reading stage they are at, there's
a Rainbow Magic book for everyone!
Here is Lydia the Reading Fairy's guide to
supporting your child's journey at all levels.

Starting Out

1

Our Rainbow Magic Beginner Readers are perfect for first-time readers who are just beginning to develop reading skills and confidence. Approved by teachers, they contain a full range of educational levelling, as well as lively full-colour illustrations.

Developing Readers

2

Rainbow Magic Early Readers contain longer stories and wider vocabulary for building stamina and growing confidence. These are adaptations of our most popular Rainbow Magic stories, specially developed for younger readers in conjunction with an Early Years reading consultant, with full-colour illustrations.

Going Solo

3

The Rainbow Magic chapter books – a mixture of series and one-off specials – contain accessible writing to encourage your child to venture into reading independently. These highly collectible and much-loved magical stories inspire a love of reading to last a lifetime.

www.rainbowmagicbooks.co.uk

"Rainbow Magic got my daughter reading chapter books. Great sparkly covers, cute fairies and traditional stories full of magic that she found impossible to put down" – Mother of Edie (6 years)

"Florence LOVES the Rainbow Magic books. She really enjoys reading now" Mother of Florence (6 years)

The Rainbow Magic Reading Challenge

Well done, fairy friend – you have completed the book!
This book was worth 5 points.

See how far you have climbed on the **Reading Rainbow**
on the Rainbow Magic website below.

The more books you read, the more points you will get,
and the closer you will be to becoming a Fairy Princess!

How to get your Reading Rainbow
1. Cut out the coin below
2. Go to the Rainbow Magic website
3. Download and print out your poster
4. Add your coin and climb up the Reading Rainbow!

There's all this and lots more at
www.rainbowmagicbooks.co.uk

You'll find activities, competitions, stories, a special
newsletter and complete profiles of all the
Rainbow Magic fairies. Find a fairy with your name!